Rixon

The Timid Little Hippo

Nancy Crosby

LifeRich Publishing is a registered trademark of The Reader's Digest Association, Inc.

LifeRich Publishing books may be ordered through booksellers or by contacting:

LifeRich Publishing
1663 Liberty Drive
Bloomington, IN 47403
www.liferichpublishing.com
1 (888) 238-8637

Because of the dynamic nature of the Internet, any web addresses or links contained in this book may have changed since publication and may no longer be valid. The views expressed in this work are solely those of the author and do not necessarily reflect the views of the publisher, and the publisher hereby disclaims any responsibility for them.

Any people depicted in stock imagery provided by Getty Images are models, and such images are being used for illustrative purposes only. Certain stock imagery © Getty Images.

ISBN: 978-1-4897-1623-1 (sc)
ISBN: 978-1-4897-1624-8 (hc)
ISBN: 978-1-4897-1622-4 (e)

Print information available on the last page.

LifeRich Publishing rev. date: 3/13/2018

Rixon

This is Rixon. He is very little for a hippopotamus. That is because he is only nine months old.

Rixon lives in Africa with his mother and father, two brothers, one sister, and twelve cousins.

Every day Rixon and his family walk to the cool river. They love to stand in the soft mud of the river bottom. They play hide-and-seek by ducking under the water. The clear, cool water feels good on their thick gray skin.

Everyone has fun except Rixon. Rixon is afraid of the water. His cousins call to him. "Come on, Rixon. Come and play with us." Rixon wants to have fun, but he is too afraid of the water. He stays on the riverbank and watches.

Day by day the sun grows hotter. Rixon grows hotter and hotter, and his thick skin begins to itch. He would like to cool off, and he would really like to stop itching, but he is still too afraid of the water.

One day, while Rixon is standing on the riverbank, he sees something shiny in the water. What could it be? Rixon looks, but he cannot tell. The shiny thing in the water is too far away.

Maybe, he thinks, *if I move just a little closer, I can see.* And Rixon walks a few steps closer to the water, but still he cannot see what the shiny thing is. He takes a few more steps. Rixon is so curious about the shiny thing that he does not realize his front feet are in the water.

Rixon looks down at the shiny thing. He sees himself. *What is this? How can it be?* he wonders. *How can I be down there if I am up here?*

Rixon is so surprised. Down goes his head into the water. He picks up the shiny thing with his teeth and takes it to the riverbank. "Oh," says Rixon. "It is only a mirror. It is not really me."

Rixon's family gathers around him. "You did it!" they shout. "You went in the water!"

"So I did! I really did," Rixon says proudly. "And I'm not afraid anymore." Now when it is time for Rixon and his family to walk to the river, who do you suppose is first in line?

CPSIA information can be obtained
at www.ICGtesting.com
Printed in the USA
BVHW020938260919
559484BV00012B/689/P

9 781489 716231